S0-AAC-998

Octavia
And Her Purple Ink Cloud

By Donna Rathmell German and
Doreen Rathmell Meredith

Illustrated by Connie McLennan

To the many generations of the Rathmell family: thanks for all the encouragement—DRG & DRM

For Karla Yaconelli: my sister, my friend, and my staunchest cheerleader—CM

Thanks to educators at the South Carolina Aquarium for verifying the accuracy of the information in this book.

Publisher's Cataloging-In-Publication Data

Octavia and her purple ink cloud / by Donna Rathmell German and Doreen Rathmell Meredith ; illustrated by Connie McLennan.

1 v. (unpaged) : col. ill. ; 27 cm.

Summary: Octavia the octopus can shoot every color of ink cloud except the usual purple one. She practices knowing that she needs the purple one to camouflage from predators. Will she be able to shoot her purple cloud when it counts? Includes For Creative Minds educational section.

ISBN: 978-0-9764943-5-5 (hardcover)
ISBN: 978-1-6071811-7-0 (pbk.)
Also available as eBooks featuring auto-flip, auto-read, 3D-page-curling, and selectable English and Spanish text and audio
Interest level: 003-007
Grade level: P-2
Lexile Level: 730 Lexile Code: AD

1. Octopuses --Juvenile fiction. 2. Perseverance (Ethics) --Juvenile fiction. 3. Octopuses --Fiction. 4.Color --Fiction. I. McLennan, Connie. II. Title.

813.6 22   2005921094

Manufactured in China, January, 2010
This product conforms to CPSIA 2008
Second Printing

Sylvan Dell Publishing
976 Houston Northcutt Blvd., Suite 3
Mt. Pleasant, SC 29464

Octavia Octopus lived alone in a small, secret cave in a colorful coral reef. She had many friends, so she was never lonely. She and her friends played a game called "how to hide from a hungry creature."

Octavia clapped all eight arms when Paul Porcupine Fish puffed up to show how he could confuse a hungry creature. He was so big and prickly that Octavia knew Paul would be safe.

Octavia bragged that she could squirt a purple ink cloud to escape. "Watch me!" she said as she squirted . . .

. . . a yellow ink cloud! "Oh no—I'd better practice," she cried.

Octavia laughed when Sandy Seahorse showed how he could hold onto a plant with his tail. He swayed in the water like he was part of the plant. She knew that he would be safe.

Octavia boasted that she could squirt a purple ink cloud to escape. She squirted . . .

. . . an orange ink cloud! "Oh no—I'd better practice," she sighed.

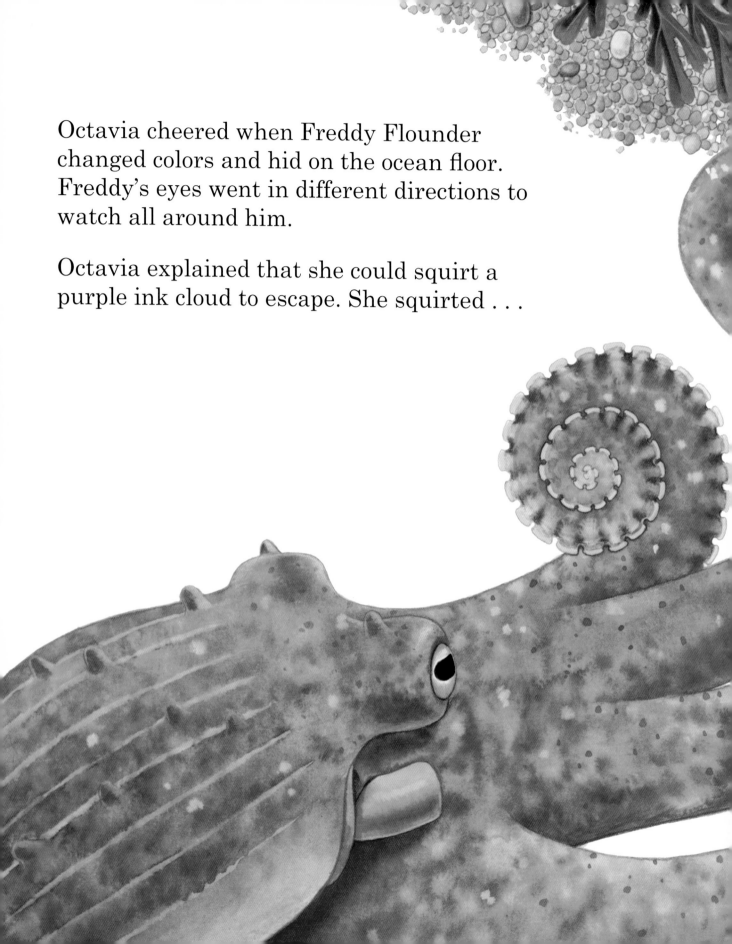

Octavia cheered when Freddy Flounder
changed colors and hid on the ocean floor.
Freddy's eyes went in different directions to
watch all around him.

Octavia explained that she could squirt a
purple ink cloud to escape. She squirted . . .

. . . a green ink cloud! "Oh no—I'd better practice," she moaned.

Octavia giggled when Greta Green Sea Turtle showed how she could hide in the grass. It was hard to see where she was.

Octavia claimed that she could squirt a purple ink cloud to escape. She squirted . . .

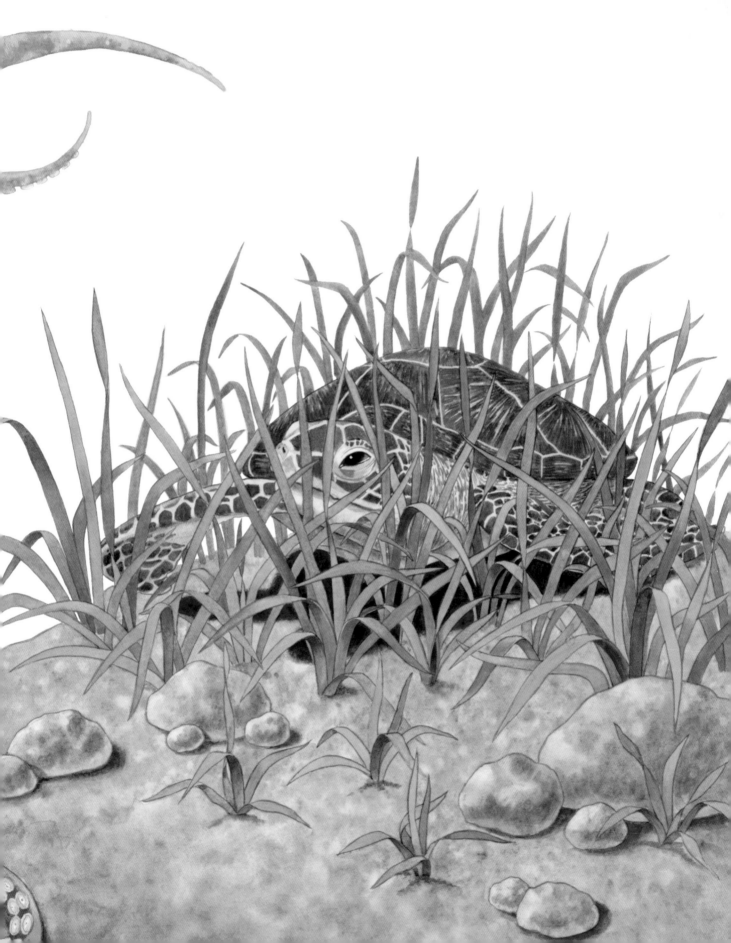

. . . a red ink cloud! "Oh no—I'd better practice," she groaned.

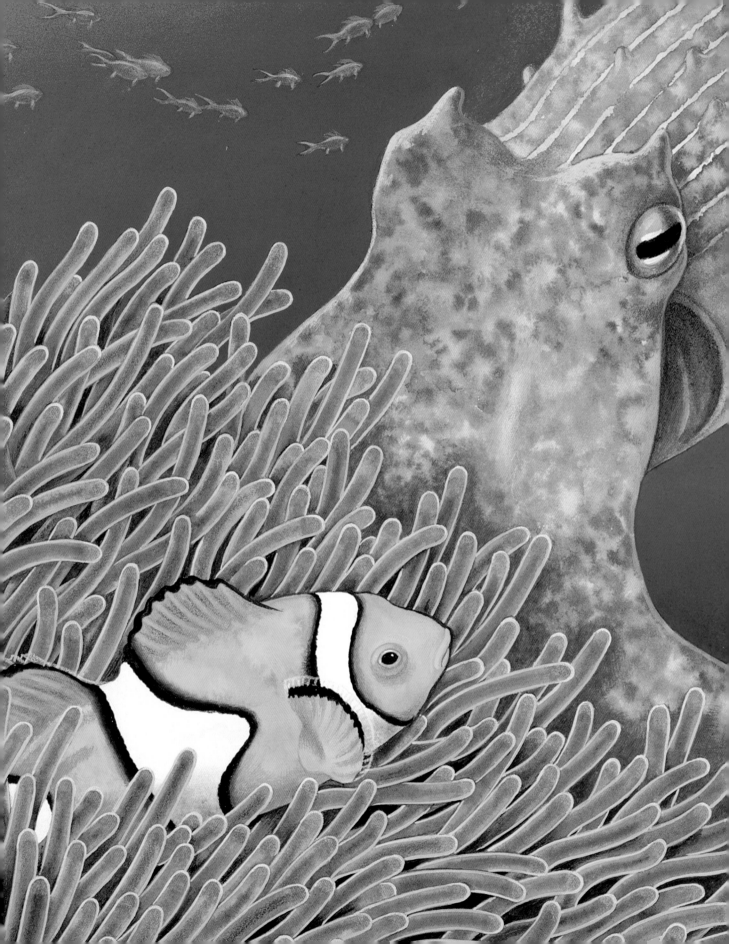

Octavia smiled when Carolyn Clown Fish showed how she could dart into a sea anemone to hide. Octavia knew that the sea anemone's stinging tentacles would help protect Carolyn.

Octavia hoped that she could squirt a purple ink cloud to escape. She squirted . . .

. . . a blue ink cloud! "Oh no—I'd better practice," she whined.

Octavia was jumping up and down as Polly Parrotfish showed how she could hide in holes of the colorful coral reef.

Just then, a great big, hungry shark swam around the reef heading right toward them!

Paul Porcupine puffed up to confuse the shark.

Sandy Seahorse held on tight to the plant.

Freddy Flounder hid on the ocean floor.

Greta Green Sea Turtle hid in the grass.

Carolyn Clownfish darted into the sea anemone.

Polly Parrotfish hid in a small hole in the reef.

Octavia turned white with fright and thought,
"I'd better squirt my purple ink cloud so I can
swim away!"

She thought very hard and squirted . . .

. . . a great big, dark, purple ink cloud! The shark could not see Octavia as she swam home to her cozy, safe cave.

"Phew," she thought. "It's a good thing I practiced!"

The great big, hungry shark swam away
with an empty belly.

For Creative Minds

Camouflage, Protection, & Adaptations—Who am I?

Animals have adaptations to help them survive in their habitats. These adaptations can be physical (body parts) or behavorial (something the animal does). Many animals use camouflage to hide from predators (animals that want to eat them) and prey (animals that they want to eat). But camouflage isn't the only way that animals protect themselves. Match the animal to its adaptations that help it to survive life in the ocean. Answers are upside down on the bottom of the next page.

1 I am the top predator of my food chain. I use my sleek body to move quickly through the water to catch prey. My underside is light colored so animals from below don't see me against light, but the top of my body is dark to blend in with the water below for animals looking down at me.

2 I have bright colors to blend in with the colorful reef where I live. I like to hide from predators in caves or crevices (cracks) in the reef.

3 I have a carapace (hard shell) to protect me from predators. My brownish-green color helps me to blend in and hide in sea grass. My flippers help me swim. Unlike some of my land cousins, I cannot pull my head into my shell.

4 I am a fish but I don't swim very well. I do have a really strong tail that I wrap around grass or corals. I can be hard to see. I use my long, narrow mouth like a vacuum cleaner to catch food as it drifts by.

5 I can change colors to match my surroundings! I use dark red, purple, or black ink clouds to confuse my enemies to escape or to catch my prey.

6 I can change the color of my skin to copy the area around me. I usually lay flat on the ground but can swim too. Both my eyes are on top of my head and can move in different directions at the same time, so I can see all around me!

7 When I get scared, I blow myself up like a balloon. I might even have quills or barbs that could stick in the throat of any predator that tries to eat me.

8 I live in a sea anemone. I have a special mucus that prevents me from getting stung. My bright color attracts other fish and they get stung. I get to eat the leftovers!

Answers: 1-shark, 2-parrot fish, 3-sea turtle, 4-seahorse, 5-octopus, 6-flounder, 7 puffer fish, 8-clown fish

Octopus Fun Facts

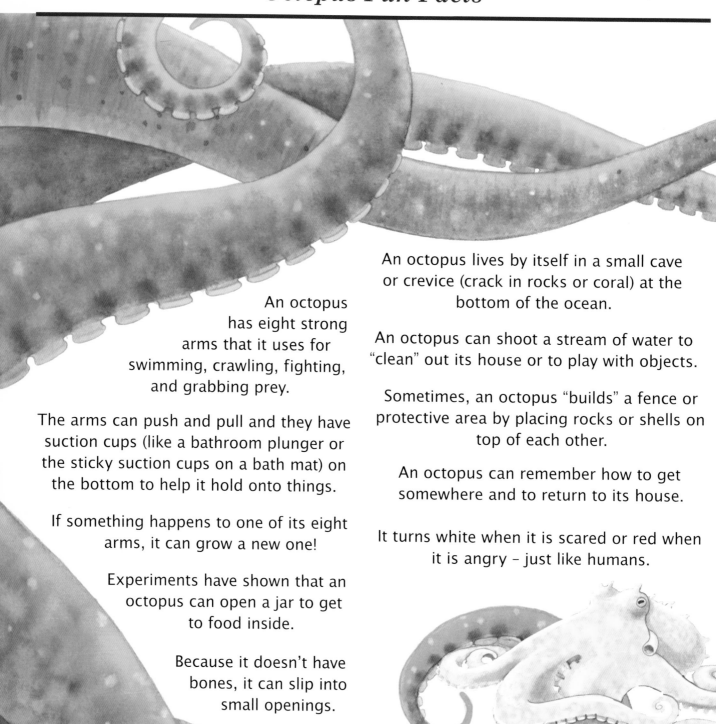

An octopus has eight strong arms that it uses for swimming, crawling, fighting, and grabbing prey.

The arms can push and pull and they have suction cups (like a bathroom plunger or the sticky suction cups on a bath mat) on the bottom to help it hold onto things.

If something happens to one of its eight arms, it can grow a new one!

Experiments have shown that an octopus can open a jar to get to food inside.

Because it doesn't have bones, it can slip into small openings.

An octopus lives by itself in a small cave or crevice (crack in rocks or coral) at the bottom of the ocean.

An octopus can shoot a stream of water to "clean" out its house or to play with objects.

Sometimes, an octopus "builds" a fence or protective area by placing rocks or shells on top of each other.

An octopus can remember how to get somewhere and to return to its house.

It turns white when it is scared or red when it is angry – just like humans.

An octopus has three hearts.